KB024644

지상에서의

A Few Days on Earth

며칠

지상에서의 며칠
A Few Days on Earth

초판 1쇄 발행 2014년 7월 14일

시 　 나태주
번역 최영의

펴낸이 김선기
펴낸곳 (주)푸른길
출판등록 1996년 4월 12일 제16-1292호
주소 (152-847) 서울시 구로구 디지털로 33길 48 대륭포스트타워 7차 1008호
전화 02-523-2907, 6942-9570-2
팩스 02-523-2951
이메일 purungilbook@naver.com
홈페이지 www.purungil.co.kr

ISBN 978-89-6291-259-3　03810

이 도서의 국립중앙도서관 출판예정도서목록(CIP)은 서지정보유통지원시스템 홈페
이지(http://seoji.nl.go.kr)와 국가자료공동목록시스템(http://www.nl.go.kr/
kolisnet)에서 이용하실 수 있습니다. (CIP제어번호: CIP2014019884)

지상에서의
A Few Days on Earth
며칠

나태주 시 · 최영의 역

Tae-Joo Ra
Translated by Young Eui Choi

푸른길

서문

한글로 시 쓰는 사람으로서 번역시집을 갖고 싶은 것은 오래 묵은 꿈 가운데 하나입니다. 그것도 최강의 국제어인 영어로 시집이 번역된다는 것은 매우 소망스러운 일 가운데 하나입니다. 이번에 다행히 최영의 교수의 번역을 만나 나의 시편들이 영역시집으로 나오게 되었습니다.

최영의 교수는 내가 사는 공주가 고향인 분으로 공주 사람의 정서와 말맛을 가장 잘 아는 한국계 미국인일 뿐더러 미국으로 건너가 본토의 영시를 공부하고 가르친 학자입니다. 그러므로 나의 시의 번역자로서는 그 어떤 사람보다도 가장 애정을 가질 수 있는 분입니다.

어려운 형편 가운데 여러 편의 시들을 아름다운 문장으로 번역해 주심에 감사드리며 이 책이 세상에 나오는 날, 우리는 한국의 하늘 아래 빛나는 웃음으로 마주 앉아 많은 이야기를 나눌 것입니다. 살면서 행운이 많고 횡재가 많은데 이 시집 또한 나에게는 행운이며 횡재입니다. 최영의 교수의 노고에 다시한 번 감사드립니다.

우리가 추운 겨울을 웅크리고 사는 것은 마음속에 봄이 숨어 있고 밝고 환한 새소리와 햇빛과 물소리가 그 속에 더불어 숨 쉬고 있음을 의심 없이 믿기 때문입니다.

2014년 공주에서, 나태주

Introduction

As a Korean poet, I have had a long dream to have my poetry book translated. Especially having it in English, the most powerful language in the world, is one of the things I have greatly hoped for. Fortunately, a collection of my poems is now at its birth in English, meeting Professor Young Eui Choi's translation.

Professor Choi's hometown is Gongju where I reside. As a Korean-American, she is not only the best one to know the sentiment and nuances of language of the folks, but also a scholar who has studied and taught English poetry in America. Thus I regard her as the most desirable translator of my poetry work.

I am grateful for her beautiful translation born in the midst of her hectic schedules. When this book is released, we will share many stories as shining smiles under the Korean sky. During our journey of life, we encounter many blessings and good fortunes, and this book is definitely one of them to me. Again, I thank Professor Choi for her endeavor to make it happen.

We endure cold winter because we believe in the hidden spring in our heart and that the bright bird songs, sunshine, and water sounds are also breathing in it without a doubt.

Tae-Joo Ra, Gongju, 2014

차 례 • *Contents*

2부

3부

지상에서의 며칠

A Few Days on Earth

제1부

Section One

시

마당을 쓸었습니다
지구 한 모퉁이가 깨끗해졌습니다

꽃 한 송이 피었습니다
지구 한 모퉁이가 아름다워졌습니다

마음속에 시 하나 싹텄습니다
지구 한 모퉁이가 밝아졌습니다

나는 지금 그대를 사랑합니다
지구 한 모퉁이가 더욱 깨끗해지고
아름다워졌습니다.

Poetry

I have swept the yard

A corner of the earth has become clean

A flower has bloomed

A corner of the earth has become beautiful

A poem has sprouted in my heart

A corner of the earth has become bright

I love you now

A corner of the earth has become more

Clean and beautiful.

풀꽃

자세히 보아야
예쁘다

오래 보아야
사랑스럽다

너도 그렇다.

Grass Flower

Pretty
With a close look

Lovely
With a long gaze

So are you.

사랑

목말라 물을 좀 마셨으면 좋겠다고
속으로 생각하고 있을 때
유리컵에 맑은 물 가득 담아
잘람잘람 내 앞으로 가지고 오는

창밖의 머언 풍경에 눈길을 주며
그리움의 물결에 몸을 맡기고 있을 때
그 물결의 흐름을 느끼고 눈물
글썽글썽한 눈으로 나를 바라보아주는

어떻게 알았을까, 그는
한마디 말씀도 이루지 아니했고
한 줌의 눈짓조차 건네지 않았음에도.

Love

While I think to myself
This thirst makes me want to drink
Bringing a full glass of clean water
In front of me

While I surrender to the waves of missing
With my gaze upon the distant view outside the window
Looking at me in tearful eyes
With the feeling of the flowing waves

How could it be, even though he
Didn't even make a remark
Didn't even give a blink of wink.

부탁

너무 멀리까지는 가지 말아라
사랑아

모습 보이는 곳까지만
목소리 들리는 곳까지만 가거라

돌아오는 길 잊을까 걱정이다
사랑아.

A Request

Don't go too far
My love

Go up to the point where I can see you
Where I can hear you

I'm afraid you will forget the way back
My love.

화이트 크리스마스

크리스마스이브
눈 내리는 늦은 밤거리에 서서
집에서 혼자 기다리고 있는
늙은 아내를 생각한다

시시하다 그럴 테지만
밤늦도록 불을 켜놓고 손님을
기다리는 빵 가게에 들러
아내가 좋아하는 빵을 몇 가지
골라 사들고 서서
한사코 세워주지 않는
택시를 기다리며
20년 하고서도 6년 동안
함께 산 동지를 생각한다

아내는 그동안 네 번
수술을 했고
나는 한 번 수술을 했다
그렇다, 아내는 네 번씩
깨진 항아리이고 나는
한 번 깨진 항아리이다

눈은 땅에 내리자마자
녹아 물이 되고 만다
목덜미에 내려 섬뜩섬뜩한
혓바닥을 들이밀기도 한다

화이트 크리스마스
크리스마스이브 늦은 밤거리에서
한 번 깨진 항아리가
네 번 깨진 항아리를 생각하며
택시를 기다리고 또
기다린다.

White Christmas

On Christmas Eve

Standing on a snowy street late at night

I think of my old wife

Who is waiting for me at home all alone

It may not be a big deal, but

I drop by a bakery that is waiting for

Customers with lights on that late

And pick up a few favorites of hers and

Think about my companion who has been living with me

For twenty plus six years

Waiting for a taxi that just passes by me

My wife has had

Four surgeries so far

I have had one

Yes, she is a clay pot

That has been broken four times and I

Am one broken once

The snow melts into water

As soon as it lands on the ground

It also intrudes the nape of my neck

With its frightening tongue

White Christmas

On the street on late Christmas Eve

A once-broken pot

Thinking of the one that has been broken four times

Is waiting and

Waiting for a taxi.

별리

우리 다시는 만나지 못하리

그대 꽃이 되고 풀이 되고
나무가 되어
내 앞에 있는다 해도 차마
그대 눈치채지 못하고

나 또한 구름 되고 바람 되고
천둥이 되어
그대 옆을 흐른다 해도 차마
나 알아보지 못하고

눈물은 번져
조그만 새암을 만든다
지구라는 별에서의
마지막 만남과 헤어짐

우리 다시 사람으로는 만나지 못하리.

A Farewell

We won't meet each other again

Even if you become a flower a grass
A tree
And stand in front of me
I still won't notice you

Even if I become a cloud a wind
A thunder
And flow beside you
You still won't recognize me

Tears spread out
And make a small well
On a star called Earth
The last encounter and farewell

We won't meet each other again as a human being.

대숲 아래서

1.
바람은 구름을 몰고
구름은 생각을 몰고
다시 생각은 대숲을 몰고
대숲 아래 내 마음은 낙엽을 몬다.

2.
밤새도록 댓잎에 별빛 어리듯
그슬린 등피에는 네 얼굴이 어리고
밤 깊어 대숲에는 후둑이다 가는 밤 소나기 소리.
그리고도 간간이 사운대다 가는 밤바람 소리.

3.
어제는 보고 싶다 편지 쓰고
어젯밤 꿈엔 너를 만나 쓰러져 울었다.
자고 나니 눈두덩엔 메마른 눈물자죽,
문을 여니 산골엔 실비단 안개.

4.

모두가 내 것만은 아닌 가을,
해 지는 서녘 구름만이 내 차지다.
동구 밖에 떠드는 애들의
소리만이 내 차지다.
또한 동구 밖에서부터 피어오르는
밤안개만이 내 차지다.

하기는 모두가 내 것만은 아닌 것도 아닌
이 가을,
저녁밥 일찍이 먹고
우물가에 산보 나온
달님만이 내 차지다.
물에 빠져 머리칼 헹구는
달님만이 내 차지다.

Under the Bamboo Trees

1.

Winds carry clouds

Clouds carry thoughts

Thoughts then carry bamboo trees

Under the bamboo trees I carry fallen leaves.

2.

All night long like the reflections of the stars on the bamboo
leaves

The reflection of your face on the smoked lampshade

The patter of a night shower in the bamboo forest deep in the
night.

And the soft sound of sporadic night breezes.

3.

Yesterday I wrote a letter to you that I missed you

And in my dream last night I met you and fell down crying.

After sleep my eyes with the marks of dried tears,

Through the open window the thin silky ray of fog in the village.

4.

In the fall not everything is mine,

Only the west cloud at sunset is what I can claim

The noise of children playing out on the street

Is what I can claim.

And the night fog rising out of the street

Is what I can claim.

Actually this fall it may not be true

That not everything is mine,

Only the moon that

Strolled out to the well

After early dinner

Is what I can claim.

Only the moon that washes its hair drowned in the water

Is what I can claim.

내가 꿈꾸는 여자

1.
내가 꿈꾸는 여자는
발가락이 이쁜 여자.
발뒤꿈치가 이쁜 여자.
발톱이 이쁜 여자.

정말로 내가 꿈꾸는 여자는
발가락에 때가 묻지 않은 여자.
발뒤꿈치에 때가 묻지 않은 여자.
발톱에 때가 묻지 않은 여자.

그리고 감옥 속에 갇혀서
다소곳이 기다릴 줄도 아는 발을 가진
그러한 여자.

2.
그녀의 발은 꽃이다.
그녀의 발은 물에서 금방 건져낸 물고기다.
그녀의 발은 풀밭에 이는 바람이다.
그녀의 발은 흰구름이다.

그녀의 발은
내 가슴을 짓이기기 위해서만 존재한다.
그녀의 발 아래서
나의 가슴은 비로소 꽃잎일 수 있다.
그녀의 발 아래서
나의 가슴은 비로소 흰구름일 수 있다.
금방 물에서 건져낸 물고기일 수도 있다.

The Woman of My Dream

1.

The woman of my dream is the one

With beautiful toes.

With beautiful heels.

With beautiful toe nails.

The woman of my real dream is the one

Without any stains in her toes.

Without any stains around her heels.

Without any stains in her toe nails.

And with a foot that can wait meekly

Confined in a jail

Such a woman.

2.

Her feet are flowers.

Her feet are fishes taken fresh from the water.

Her feet are winds waving on the grass field.

Her feet are white clouds.

Her feet

Only exist to crush my chest.

Beneath her feet

My chest can finally become a petal.

Beneath her feet

My chest can finally become a white cloud.

It can also become a fish fresh from the water.

사랑하는 마음 내게 있어도

사랑하는 마음
내게 있어도
사랑한다는 말
차마 건네지 못하고 삽니다
사랑한다는 그 말 끝까지
감당할 수 없기 때문

모진 마음
내게 있어도
모진 말
차마 하지 못하고 삽니다
나도 모진 말 남들한테 들으면
오래오래 잊혀지지 않기 때문

외롭고 슬픈 마음
내게 있어도
외롭고 슬프다는 말
차마 하지 못하고 삽니다
외롭고 슬픈 말 남들한테 들으면
나도 덩달아 외롭고 슬퍼지기 때문

사랑하는 마음을 아끼며
삽니다
모진 마음을 달래며
삽니다
될수록 외롭고 슬픈 마음을
숨기며 삽니다.

Even with This Love for You

Even with this
Love for you
I love you
Are the words still hard for me to say
'Cause I can't hold on to the words
Until the end

Even with this
Harsh mind
Harsh words
Are the ones still hard for me to say
'Cause when I hear them from others
I will remember them for a long long time

Even with this

Lonely and sad heart

I'm lonely and sad

Are the words still hard for me to say

'Cause when I hear lonely and sad words from others

I get lonely and sad as well

I live

Saving my loving heart

I live

Consoling my harsh mind

I live

Hiding my lonely and sad heart as much as possible.

비단강

비단강이 비단강임은
많은 강을 돌아보고 나서야
비로소 알겠습니다

그대가 내게 소중한 사람임은
더 많은 사람들을 만나고 나서야
비로소 알겠습니다

백 년을 가는
사람 목숨이 어디 있으며
오십 년을 가는
사람 사랑이 어디 있으랴……

오늘도 나는
강가를 지나며
되뇌어 봅니다.

Silk River

Silk River is Silk River
I finally realize it
After visiting many rivers

You are a precious person
I finally realize it
After meeting many people

Where is a human life
Longer than a hundred years
Where is a human love
Longer than fifty years...

Today I
Whisper to myself
Passing by the river.

완성

집에 밥이 있어도 나는
아내 없으면 밥을 먹지 않는 사람

내가 데려다 주지 않으면 아내는
서울 딸네 집에도 가지 못하는 사람

우리는 이렇게 함께 살면서
반편이 인간으로 완성되고 말았다.

Completion

I'm a man who doesn't even eat a meal at home
If my wife isn't there

My wife is a woman who can't even go to our daughter's in
Seoul
If I don't take her there

Living together like this
A half of us has been complete as a whole person.

오늘의 약속

덩치 큰 이야기, 무거운 이야기는 하지 않기로 해요
조그만 이야기, 가벼운 이야기만 하기로 해요
아침에 일어나 낯선 새 한 마리가 날아가는 것을 보았다든지
길을 가다 담장 너머 아이들 떠들며 노는 소리가 들려 잠시 발을
멈췄다든지
매미 소리가 하늘 속으로 강물을 만들며 흘러가는 것을 문득 느
꼈다든지
그런 이야기들만 하기로 해요

남의 이야기, 세상 이야기는 하지 않기로 해요
우리들의 이야기, 서로의 이야기만 하기로 해요
지나간 밤 쉽게 잠이 오지 않아 애를 먹었다든지
하루 종일 보고픈 마음이 떠나지 않아 가슴이 뻐근했다든지
모처럼 개인 밤하늘 사이로 별 하나 찾아내어 숨겨놓은 소원을
빌었다든지
그런 이야기들만 하기로 해요

실은 우리들 이야기만 하기에도 시간이 많지 않은 걸 우리는 잘
알아요
그래요, 우리 멀리 떨어져 살면서도
오래 헤어져 살면서도 스스로
행복해지기로 해요
그게 오늘의 약속이에요.

Today's Promise

A huge story, let's not talk about a heavy story
A small story, let's just talk about a light story
Like the ones that
You got up in the morning and saw an unfamiliar bird flying
You paused briefly while walking on the road
Hearing children's playing over the fence
You suddenly felt the sound of cicadas
Flowing into the sky as a river

Gossips about others, let's not talk about the worldly stories
Our stories, let's just talk about ourselves
Like the ones that
You had a hard time falling asleep last night
You had an achy heart with immense missing all day long
You found a star in the unusually clear night sky and
Made a secret wish

Actually we know well that

Time is not enough even just for our stories

Yeah, even if we live far apart

Even if we are long separated from each other

Let's try to be happy with ourselves

That's today's promise.

다리 위에서

너는 바람 속에 피어
웃고 있는 가을꽃

눈을 감아 본다

흐르는 강물은 보이지 않고
키 큰 가로등도 보이지 않고
너의 맑은 이마도 보이지 않는다

그러나 여전히
강물은 흐르고
가로등 불빛은 밝고
너의 이마 또한 내 앞에 있었으리라

눈을 떠 본다

너는 새로 돋아나기 시작하는
초저녁 밤별.

On the Bridge

You are a smiling autumn flower
Open in the winds

I close my eyes

The flowing river is not seen
The tall street lamp is not seen any more
Nor your lucid forehead

Still
The river must have been flowing
The street lamp must have been bright
And your forehead must have been in front of me

I open my eyes

You are an early evening star
Just now rising up.

산수유꽃 진 자리

사랑한다, 나는 사랑을 가졌다
누구에겐가 말해주긴 해야 했는데
마음 놓고 말해줄 사람 없어
산수유꽃 옆에 와 무심히 중얼거린 소리
노랗게 핀 산수유꽃이 외워두었다가
따사로운 햇빛한테 들려주고
놀러 온 산새에게 들려주고
시냇물 소리한테까지 들려주어
사랑한다, 나는 사랑을 가졌다
차마 이름까진 말해줄 수 없어 이름만 빼고
알려준 나의 말
여름 한 철 시냇물이 줄창 외우며 흘러가더니
이제 가을도 저물어 시냇물 소리도 입을 다물고
다만 산수유꽃 진 자리 산수유 열매들만
내리는 눈발 속에 더욱 예쁘고 붉습니다.

Where the yellow dogwoods fell

I love you, I have love

I had to say that to somebody

But didn't have anybody to say it to

So whispered it mindlessly by the yellow dogwoods

Then they remembered it and

Relayed it to the warm sunlight

To the mountain birds stopping by

Even to the sound of the stream

I love you, I have love

I let it out without the name

'Cause I couldn't tell the name

All summer long the stream was flowing reciting it

Now in the late fall the sound of stream has closed its lips

Only the fruits of the yellow dogwoods where the flowers fell

Are prettier and redder in the flurry of snow.

꽃잎

활짝 핀 꽃나무 아래서
우리는 만나서 웃었다

눈이 꽃잎이었고
이마가 꽃잎이었고
입술이 꽃잎이었다

우리는 술을 마셨다
눈물을 글썽이기도 했다

사진을 찍고
그날 그렇게 우리는
헤어졌다

돌아와 사진을 빼보니
꽃잎만 찍혀 있었다.

Petals

Under a fully blossomed flower tree
We met and smiled

Our eyes were petals
Our foreheads were petals
Our lips were petals

We drank wine together
Tears welled up in our eyes, too

After taking a picture
That day like that we
Said good bye

Then in the photo developed
Were only the petals.

돌계단

네 손을 잡고 돌계단을 오르고 있었지.

돌계단 하나에 석등이 보이고
돌계단 둘에 석탑이 보이고
돌계단 셋에 극락전이 보이고
극락전 뒤에 푸른 산이 다가서고
하늘에는 흰구름이 돛을 달고 마악
떠나가려 하고 있었지.

하늘이 보일 때 이미
돌계단은 끝이 나 있었고
내 손에 이끌려 돌계단을 오르던 너는
이미 내 옆에 없었지.

홀쩍 하늘로 날아가 흰구름이 되어버린 너!

우리는 모두 흰구름이에요, 흰구름.
육신을 벗고 나면 이렇게 가볍게 빛나는
당신이나 저나 흰구름일 뿐이에요.
너는 하늘 속에서 나를 보며 어서 오라 손짓하며 웃고
나는 너를 따라갈 수 없어 땅에서 울고 있었지.
발을 구르며 땅에 서서 울고만 있었지.

Stone Steps

I was climbing on stone steps holding your hands.

On one step appeared a stone lantern
On two steps appeared a stone pagoda
On three steps appeared Paradise Dharma Hall
Behind the Paradise Dharma Hall emerged a blue mountain
In the sky white clouds
Were about to leave with a sail.

When the sky came into the view
The stone steps had already reached the end
You who were accompanying me led by my hands
Had already disappeared.

You who swiftly flew into the sky and became a white cloud!

We are all white clouds, white clouds.

After taking off flesh, shining light like this

You and I are just white clouds.

You were beckoning me with a smile from the sky

I was crying on the ground unable to follow you.

Just crying tapping my feet on the ground.

제2부

Section Two

행복

저녁 때
돌아갈 집이 있다는 것

힘들 때
마음속으로 생각할 사람 있다는 것

외로울 때
혼자서 부를 노래 있다는 것.

Happiness

In the evening
Having a home to return

In difficult times
Having a soul to recall in the heart

In lonely times
Having a song to sing alone.

선물

하늘 아래 내가 받은
가장 커다란 선물은
오늘입니다

오늘 받은 선물 가운데서도
가장 아름다운 선물은
당신입니다

당신 나지막한 목소리와
웃는 얼굴, 콧노래 한 구절이면
한 아름 바다를 안은 듯한 기쁨이겠습니다.

Gift

Under the sky
The biggest gift I've received
Is today

Out of the gifts
I've received today
The most beautiful gift
Is you

Your soft voice,
Smiling face, a note of humming
Give me a delight
Like an embrace of the ocean.

서정시인

다른 아이들 모두 서커스 구경 갈 때
혼자 남아 집을 보는 아이처럼
모로 돌아서서 까치집을 바라보는
늙은 화가처럼
신도들한테 따돌림당한
시골 목사처럼.

A Lyric Poet

Like a kid who is left alone at home

While other kids all go to a circus

Like an old painter who turns around and

Gazes at a magpie nest

Like a country priest

Who is alienated by his congregation.

서울, 하이에나

결코 사냥하지 않는다

먹다 남긴 고기를 훔치고
썩은 고기도 마다하지 않는다
어찌 고기를 훔치는 발톱이
고독을 안다 하겠는가?
썩은 고기를 찢는 이빨이
슬픔을 어찌 안다고 말하겠는가?

딸아, 사냥하기 싫거든
차라리 서울서
굶다가 죽어라.

Seoul, Hyena

Never hunts

Steals leftover meat
Doesn't even mind rotten meat
How could the meat-stealing claw
Know solitude?
How could the rotten-meat-tearing teeth
Know sorrow?

My daughter, if you don't want to hunt
You'd better starve to death
In Seoul.

유리창

이제
떠나갈 것은 떠나게 하고
남을 것은 남게 하자

혼자서 맞이하는 저녁과
혼자서 바라보는 들판을
두려워하지 말자

아, 그렇다
할 수만 있다면
나뭇잎 떨어진 빈 나뭇가지에
까마귀 한 마리라도 불러
가슴속에 기르자

이제
지나온 그림자를 지우지 못해 안달하지도 말고
다가올 날의 해짧음을 아쉬워하지도 말자.

Window

Now
Let them go if they need
Let them stay if they need

Let's not be afraid of
The evening greeted alone
The field viewed alone

Ah, yes
If possible
Let's beckon a crow
To a bare branch and
Grow it in the heart

Now
Let's not fret over erasing the past shadow
Let's not lament the shortening sun.

꽃이 되어 새가 되어

지고 가기 힘겨운 슬픔 있거든
꽃들에게 맡기고

부리기도 버거운 아픔 있거든
새들에게 맡긴다

날마다 하루해는 사람들을 비껴서
강물 되어 저만큼 멀어지지만

들판 가득 꽃들은 피어서 붉고
하늘가로 스치는 새들도 본다.

As a Flower as a Bird

If there's unbearable sorrow too difficult to carry
Leave it to flowers

If there's such pain too heavy to bear
Leave it to birds

Although the daily sun passing by people
Disappears far as a river

Field-full flowers blossom in crimson
And the birds touch the edge of the sky.

명멸

하늘에서 별 하나 사라졌다
성냥개비 하나 타오를 만큼
짧은 시간의 명멸

사람들 꿈꾸며 바라보던 그 별이다
아이들도 바라보며 노래하던 그 별이다

누구도 슬퍼하지 않았다
울지 않았다
다만 몇 사람 시무룩히
고개 숙였다 들었을 뿐이다.

Exquisite Extinction

In the sky a star has disappeared
A short extinction
Enough for a match to be in a flame

That's the star people watched while dreaming
That's the star even children sang while watching

No one was in grief
No one cried
Just a few people sullenly
Dropped their heads and lifted.

희망

날이 개면 시장에 가리라
새로 산 자전거를 타고
힘들여 페달을 비비며

될수록 소로길을 찾아서
개울길을 따라서
흐드러진 코스모스 꽃들
새로 피어나는 과꽃들 보며 가야지

아는 사람을 만나면 자전거에서 내려
악수를 청하며 인사를 할 것이다
기분이 좋아지면 휘파람이라도 불 것이다

어느 집 담장 위엔가
넝쿨콩도 올라와 열렸네
석류도 바깥세상이 궁금한지
고개 내밀고 얼굴 붉혔네

시장에 가서는
아내가 부탁한 반찬거리를 사리라
생선도 사고 채소도 사 가지고 오리라.

Hope

I shall go to the market when the day breaks
On a new bicycle
Pedaling hard

I shall go trying to find narrow roads
Along the paths by the stream
Looking at the wavy cosmos
New blossoms of china asters

I shall get off the bicycle when I see a familiar face
And greet him shaking hands
Even blow a whistle when I feel jolly

On somebody's fence

Crawling open bean vines

And pomegranates curious of the outer world

Popping out their faces in blush

At the market

I shall buy the ingredients for side dishes my wife requested

I shall also bring fishes and vegetables.

선종

피
한 방울
놓쳐버린 바다

울며
떠난 고래는
돌아오지 않았다

다만 노을이 붉었다.

Mors bona, mors sancta

A drop

Of blood

Lost from the sea

Crying

As leaving

The whale hasn't returned

Only the sunset was scarlet.

시간

누군가 한 사람 창가에 앉아
울먹이고 있다
햇빛이 스러지기 전에 떠나야 한다고
한 번 가선 돌아올 수 없는 길을
가야만 한다고
그 곳은 아주 먼 곳이라고
조그만 소리로 속삭이고 있다
잠시만 더 나와 함께 여기
머물다 갈 수는 없나요?
손이라도 잡아주고 싶어 손을 내밀었을 때
이미 그의 손은 보이지 않았다.

Time

Someone sitting by the window

Is weeping

Whispering in a low voice

Gotta leave before the sunlight falls down

Gotta go to the place

Where return is impossible once gone

Somewhere far away

Can you stay here with me a little longer

Before you go?

As my hands reached his to hold

His hands have already disappeared.

좋은 약

큰 병 얻어 중환자실에 널부러져 있을 때
아버지 절룩거리는 두 다리로 지팡이 짚고
어렵사리 면회 오시어
한 말씀, 하시었다

애야, 너는 어려서부터 몸은 약했지만
독한 아이였다
네 독한 마음으로 부디 병을 이기고 나오너라
세상은 아직도 징글징글하도록 좋은 곳이란다

아버지 말씀이 약이 되었다
두 번째 말씀이 더욱
좋은 약이 되었다.

Good Remedy

When I was helplessly lying down in an intensive care bed
Father came to see me limping his legs with a walking stick
A difficult visit
A word of wisdom, he gave

Son, even if you have been prone to illness since childhood
You have been a strong boy
With your fierce mind, please come out of the disease
The world is still an awfully good place

His words have become a good remedy
The second remark made
A better medicine.

너무 그러지 마시어요

너무 그러지 마시어요. 너무 섭섭하게 그러지 마시어요. 하나님, 저에게가 아니에요. 저의 아내 되는 여자에게 그렇게 하지 말아달라는 말씀이에요. 이 여자는 젊어서부터 병과 더불어 약과 더불어 산 여자예요. 세상에 대한 꿈도 없고 그 어떤 사람보다도 죄를 안 만든 여자예요. 신장에 구두도 많지 않은 여자구요, 장롱에 비싸고 좋은 옷도 여러 벌 가지지 못한 여자예요. 한 남자의 아내로서 그림자로 살았고 두 아이의 엄마로서 울면서 기도하는 능력밖엔 없는 여자이지요. 자기 이름으로 꽃밭 한 평, 채전밭 한 귀퉁이 가지지 못한 여자예요. 남편 되는 사람이 운전조차 할 줄 모르는 쑥맥이라서 언제나 버스만 타고 다닌 여자예요. 돈을 아끼느라 꽤나 먼 시장 길도 걸어다니고 싸구려 미장원에만 골라 다닌 여자예요. 너무 그러지 마시어요. 가난한 자의 기도를 잘 들어 응답해주시는 하나님, 저의 아내 되는 사람에게 너무 섭섭하게 그러지 마시어요.

Please don't be so cruel

Please don't be so cruel. Please don't be so heartless. My Lord, I don't mean it to me. I mean not to my wife. This woman has lived with illnesses and medicines. She doesn't have a dream for the world, nor has she made any sins. She doesn't own many pairs of shoes, nor does she have plenty of expensive clothes in her closet. She only knows how to make tearful prayers as a shadow of her husband and a mother of two children. She has no flower garden or a corner vegetable bed under her name. Since her husband is an odd ball who doesn't even know how to drive, she always rides a bus. She is a woman who walks to a faraway market and only goes to a cheap beauty parlor to save money. Please don't be so cruel. My Lord, who faithfully answers to the prayers of the poor, please don't be so heartless to my wife.

울던 자리

여기가 셋이서 울던 자리예요
저기도 셋이서 울던 자리예요
그리고 저기는 주저앉아
기도하던 자리고요

병원 로비에서
복도에서
의자 위에서
그냥 맨바닥 위에서

준비 안 된 가족과의 헤어짐이
너무나도 힘겨워서
가장의 죽음 앞에 한꺼번에 무너져서

여러 날 그들은
비를 맞아 날 수 없는
세 마리의 산비둘기였을 것이다.

Where they cried

Here is where the three cried
There is also where the three cried
And over there is where they prayed
Sitting on the ground

In the hospital lobby
In the hallway
In a chair
Just on the floor

'Cause it was too hard
To bid farewell to the unprepared family
'Cause they collapsed at once in front of the family head

For many days they
Might have been three wet mountain pigeons
Unable to fly soaked in rain.

지상에서의 며칠

때 절은 조이 창문 흐릿한 달빛 한 줌이었다가
바람 부는 들판의 키 큰 미루나무 잔가지 흔드는 바람이었다가
차마 소낙비일 수 있었을까? 겨우
옷자락이나 머리칼 적시는 이슬비였다가
기약 없이 찾아든 바닷가 민박집 문지방까지 밀려와
칭얼대는 파도 소리였다가
누군들 안 그러랴
잠시 머물고 떠나는 지상에서의 며칠, 이런 저런 일들
좋았노라 슬펐노라 고달팠노라
그대 만나 잠시 가슴 부풀고 설렜었지
그리고는 오래고 긴 적막과 애달픔과 기다림이 거기 있었지
가는 여름 새끼손톱에 스며든 봉숭아 빠알간 물감이었다가
잘려 나간 손톱조각에 어른대는 첫눈이었다가
눈물이 고여서였을까? 눈썹
깜짝이다가 눈썹 두어 번 깜짝이다가……

A Few Days on Earth

As a handful of dim moonlight on a filthy rice paper window

As a wind shaking small branches of a tall poplar on a windy field

Even as a shower? Just

As a drizzly rain wetting hair and clothes

As the sound of whining waves

Sliding into the doorstep of a seaside inn randomly reached

Who wouldn't be

Just a few days on earth before leaving, various things

Were good sad troubled

Meeting you brought me short moments of excitement and anticipation

Along with long silence sorrow and waiting

As the red paint of balsam smeared into the pinky finger nail in the passing summer

As the flurry first snow on the broken piece of the nail

Tears welled up in my eyes? As the eyebrows

As the eyebrows that blink a couple of times...

사는 일

1.
오늘도 하루 잘 살았다
굽은 길은 굽게 가고
곧은 길은 곧게 가고

막판에는 나를 싣고
가기로 되어 있는 차가
제 시간보다 일찍 떠나는 바람에
걷지 않아도 좋은 길을 두어 시간
땀 흘리며 걷기도 했다

그러나 그것도 나쁘지 아니했다
걷지 않아도 좋은 길을 걸었으므로
만나지 못했을 뻔했던 싱그러운
바람도 만나고 수풀 사이
빨갛게 익은 멍석딸기도 만나고
해 저문 개울가 고기비늘 찍으러 온 물총새
물총새, 쪽빛 날갯짓도 보았으므로

이제 날 저물려 한다
길바닥을 떠돌던 바람은 잠잠해지고
새들도 머리를 숲으로 돌렸다
오늘도 하루 나는 이렇게
잘 살았다.

2.
세상에 나를 던져보기로 한다
한 시간이나 두 시간

퇴근 버스를 놓친 날 아예
다음 차 기다리는 일을 포기해버리고
길바닥에 나를 놓아버리기로 한다

누가 나를 주워가 줄 것인가?
만약 주워가 준다면 얼마나 내가
나의 길을 줄였을 때
주워가 줄 것인가?

한 시간이나 두 시간
시험 삼아 세상 한복판에
나를 던져보기로 한다

나는 달리는 차들이 비껴 가는
길바닥의 작은 돌멩이.

Living

1.

Today I lived well

Going winding on a winding road

Going straight on a straight road

At the end the bus

That was supposed to pick me up

Left earlier than its schedule

So I had to walk in sweat for a couple of hours

On the road that I didn't have to be on

But it was not too bad

As I walked on the road that I didn't need to be on

I got to meet the fresh winds

That I could not have met otherwise and in the bushes

Wild strawberries ripe in red

Also got to see a kingfisher that came to pick fish scales by the

stream at dusk

A kingfisher, its turquoise flapping of wings

It's getting dark

The winds that were wandering on the street have waned now

and

The birds have turned their heads towards the forest

Today I lived well

Like this.

2.

Out to the world I try to cast myself

For an hour or two

On a day I miss a bus from work

I just give up on waiting for the next bus and

Leave myself on the street

Who is going to claim me?

If so, how much shrinking of

The road I need

To be claimed?

For an hour or two

As a test into the center of the world

I try to cast myself

I am a small stone on the street

Passing cars try to avoid.

기도

내가 외로운 사람이라면
나보다 더 외로운 사람을
생각하게 하여 주옵소서

내가 추운 사람이라면
나보다 더 추운 사람을
생각하게 하여 주옵소서

내가 가난한 사람이라면
나보다 더 가난한 사람을
생각하게 하여 주옵소서

더욱이나 내가 비천한 사람이라면
나보다 더 비천한 사람을
생각하게 하여 주옵소서

그리하여 때때로
스스로 묻고
스스로 대답하게 하여 주옵소서

나는 지금 어디에 와 있는가?
나는 지금 어디로 향해 가고 있는가?
나는 지금 무엇을 보고 있는가?
나는 지금 무엇을 꿈꾸고 있는가?

A Prayer

If I am a lonely man
Please let me think about
A lonelier man than me

If I am a cold man
Please let me think about
A colder man than me

If I am a poor man
Please let me think about
A poorer man than me

Moreover if I am a lowly man
Please let me think about
A lowlier man than me

So from time to time

Please let me ask myself and

Answer on my own

Where am I now?

Where am I heading now?

What am I looking at now?

What am I dreaming now?

뒤를 돌아보며

가다가, 바람보다 빨리
가다가 문득 뒤를 바라본다
발밑에 붉은 꽃
다만 이름을 버리고 붉은 꽃

가다가, 바람보다 먼저
가다가 돌아서서 바라본다
안개에 싸인 산
산에 묻힌 또 새소리

아, 니들이 나를 불렀구나
나를 불러 세웠구나

나보다 더 빠르게 간 그는
지금 어디쯤 멈춰 서서
뒤를 돌아보며 내가 오기를
기다리고 있는 걸까?

Looking back

On my way, faster than winds
On my way I look back all of a sudden
The red flowers under my feet
Just red flowers without a name

On my way, earlier than winds
On my way, I turn around and look at
The mountain in the fog and
The sound of birds buried in the mountain

Ah, you folks have called me
And stopped me

The one who went faster than me
Where has he stopped now
Looking back
Waiting for me?

악수

가을 햇살은
모든 것들을 익어가게 한다
그 품 안에 들면 산이며 들
강물이며 하다못해 곡식이며 과일
곤충 한 마리 물고기 한 마리까지
익어가지 않고서는 배겨나지를 못한다

그리하여 마을의 집들이며 담장
마을로 뚫린 꼬불길조차
마악 빵 기계에서 구워낸 빵처럼
말랑말랑하고 따스하다

몇 해 만인가 골목길에서 마주친
동갑내기 친구
나이보다 늙어 보이는 얼굴
나는 친구에게
늙었다는 표현을 삼가기로 한다

이 사람 그동안 아주 잘 익었군
무슨 말을 하는지 몰라
잠시 어리둥절해진 친구의 손을 잡는다
그의 손아귀가 무척 든든하다
역시 거칠지만 잘 구워진 빵이다.

Handshakes

The autumn sunbeam

Ripens everything

In its arms mountains fields

Rivers even grains and fruits

Even an insect and a fish

Cannot help but ripen

Then village houses and fences

Even a winding road to the village

Are soft and warm

Like fresh bread from an oven

A friend of mine of same age whom

I bump into in an alley after some years

Whose face looks older than his age

I try not to say to him

You've aged, my friend

You've been ripe quite well, my man

He doesn't get what I say

So I hold the puzzled friend's hands

His grab is quite firm

Also rough but well baked bread.

제3부

Section Three

한밤중에

한밤중에
까닭 없이
잠이 깨었다

우연히 방안의
화분에 눈길이 갔다

바짝 말라 있는 화분

어, 너였구나
네가 목이 말라 나를
깨웠구나.

At Midnight

At midnight
I woke up
For no reason

Happened to see
A flowerpot in the room

All dried out

Uh, it was you
Who woke me up
Out of thirst.

여행

집 떠난 제가 외로우니
산 위에 걸린 구름도
외롭다

아는 사람 없는 낯선 거리
길가에 피어 있는 붉은 꽃도
서럽다

강물 거울에 몸 부리고 가는
새야 새, 너
허물 벗으며 어디로 가니?

Voyage

As I feel lonely leaving home
The clouds over the mountain
Are lonely, too

Unfamiliar streets without knowing anybody
Even the red flowers by the road
Are sorrowful

Bird, bird,
Reflecting on the river mirror
Where are you going shedding off the skin?

황홀

시시각각 물이 말라 졸아붙는 웅덩이를
본 일이 있을 것이다
오직 웅덩이를 천국으로 알고 살아가던
송사리 몇 마리
파닥파닥 튀어 오르다가 뒤채다가
끝내는 잠잠해지는 몸짓
송사리 엷은 비늘에 어리어 파랗게
무지개를 세우던 햇빛, 그 황홀.

Rapture

You probably have seen a pond

That dries out to the bottom moment by moment

A few minnows

That knew the pond as the heaven only

Leap rapidly tossing and turning

And become silent after all

Reflected on the thin scales of the minnows

The sunshine that raised a rainbow blue, the rapture.

나무를 위한 예의

나무한테 찡그린 얼굴로 인사하지 마세요
나무한테 화낸 목소리로 말을 걸지 마세요
나무는 꾸중 들을 일을 하나도 하지 않았답니다
나무는 화낼 만한 일을 조금도 하지 않았답니다

나무네 가족의 가훈은 〈정직과 실천〉입니다
그리고 〈기다림〉이기도 합니다
봄이 되면 어김없이 싹을 내밀고 꽃을 피우고 또 열매 맺어 가을
을 맞고
겨울이면 옷을 벗어버린 채 서서 봄을 기다릴 따름이지요

나무의 집은 하늘이고 땅이에요
그건 나무의 어머니 어머니, 어머니 때부터의 기인 역사이지요
그 무엇도 욕심껏 가지는 일이 없고 모아두는 일도 없답니다
있는 것만큼 고마워하고 받은 만큼 덜어낼 줄 안답니다

나무한테 속상한 얼굴을 보여주지 마세요
나무한테 어두운 목소리로 투정하지 마세요
그건 나무한테 하는 예의가 아니랍니다.

Respect for a tree

Don't greet a tree with a sullen face
Don't talk to a tree in an angry voice
The tree didn't do anything to be scolded for
The tree didn't do anything to evoke anger

The family motto of the tree is <Honesty and Action>
And <Waiting>, too
In the spring it never fails to sprout out and blossom
And greets fall bearing fruits
In the winter it waits for spring standing naked

The house of the tree is the sky and the earth
That's a long history from its mother, mother, and mother
It doesn't possess or hoard things in greed
It appreciates what is there and gives out as much as it receives

Don't show your long face to the tree
Don't whine to the tree in a gloomy voice
That's not how you respect the tree.

앉은뱅이꽃

발밑에 가여운 것
밟지 마라,
그 꽃 밟으면 귀양간단다
그 꽃 밟으면 죄받는단다.

Viola

The poor thing beneath the foot

Don't crush it

If you crush the flower, you will be exiled

If you crush the flower, you will be punished.

기쁨

난초 화분의 휘어진
이파리 하나가
허공에 몸을 기댄다

허공도 따라서 휘어지면서
난초 이파리를 살그머니
보듬어 안는다

그들 사이에 사람인 내가 모르는
잔잔한 기쁨의
강물이 흐른다.

Joy

A bent leaf
of an orchid pot
leans against the air

The air also bending
quitely embraces
the orchid leaf

Between them unknown to a man
flows a river
of gentle bliss.

촉

무심히 지나치는
골목길

두껍고 단단한
아스팔트 각질을 비집고
솟아오르는
새싹의 촉을 본다

얼랄라
저 여리고
부드러운 것이!

한 개의 촉 끝에
지구를 들어 올리는
힘이 숨어 있다.

A Tip

On an aimless
Alley

I see a tip of a bud
Sprouting out
Through the callus of
Thick and hard asphalt

Oh, my, how could
Such a fragile and
Soft one!

On a tip of a bud
Is the hidden power
That lifts up the earth.

강물과 나는

맑은 날
강가에 나아가
바가지로
강물에 비친
하늘 한 자락
떠올렸습니다

물고기 몇 마리
흰구름 한 송이
새소리도 몇 움큼
건져 올렸습니다

한참 동안 그것들을
가지고 돌아오다가
생각해보니
아무래도 믿음이
서지 않았습니다

이것들을
기르다가 공연스레
죽이기라도 하면
어떻게 하나

나는 걸음을 돌려
다시 강가로 나아가
그것들을 강물에
풀어 넣었습니다

물고기와 흰구름과
새소리 모두
강물에게
돌려주었습니다

그날부터
강물과 나는
친구가 되었습니다.

The River and I

On a clear day

I went to a river and

With a gourd

Scooped up

A slice of sky

Reflected on the river

A few fishes

A bud of white cloud

And a handful of bird songs

I raised, too

Returning with these

For a long while

As I thought about it

It didn't seem like

A good idea

What if

I kill them

While growing

For nothing

I turned around and

Went out to the river

To release them

Into the water

The fishes and the white clouds

And the bird songs

I returned them all

To the water

Since that day

The river and I

Have become friends.

가을 서한 · 1

1.
끝내 빈손 들고 돌아온 가을아,
종이 기러기 한 마리 안 날아오는 비인 가을아,
내 마음까지 모두 주어버리고 난 지금
나는 또 그대에게 무엇을 주어야 할까 몰라.

2.
새로 국화잎새 따다 수놓아
새로 창호지문 바르고 나면
방안 구석구석까지 밀려들어오는 저승의 햇살.
그것은 가난한 사람들만의 겨울 양식.

3.
다시는 더 생각하지 않겠다,
다짐하고 내려오는 등성이에서
돌아보니 타닥타닥 영그는 가을 꽃씨 몇 옴큼.
바람 속에 흩어지는 산 너머 기적 소리.

4.
가을은 가고
남은 건
바바리코트 자락에 날리는 바람
때 묻은 와이셔츠 깃.

가을은 가고
남은 건
그대 만나러 가는 골목길에서의
내 휘파람 소리.

첫눈 내리는 날에
켜질
그대 창문의 등불빛
한 초롱.

Autumn Letter • 1

1.

Autumn, you are back with empty hands after all,

Autumn, you void one even a paper wild goose doesn't fly into

After giving all my heart to you

I don't know what else to give you now.

2.

After adorning the new rice paper door

With an embroidery of new chrysanthemums leaves

The sunlight of death invading every corner of the room.

That's the winter food only for the poor.

3.

I won't think any more,

With this promise coming down the mountain ridge

Behind my back a few fistful of ripe cracking of autumn flower seeds.

The sound of train whistle over the mountain dispersing into the winds.

4.

Autumn is gone
What's left
Is the wind blowing by the edge of a trench coat
The collar of a stained Y-shirt.

Autumn is gone
What's left
Is the sound of my whistle
In the alley on my way to meet you.

The lamp light on your window
That will be turned on
On a first snowy day
A lantern.

가을 서한 · 2

1.
당신도 쉽사리 건져주지 못할 슬픔이라면
해질녘 바닷가에 나와 서 있겠습니다.
금방 등돌리며 이별하는 햇볕들을 만나기 위하여.
그 햇볕들과 두 번째의 이별을 갖기 위하여.

2.
눈 한 번 감았다 뜰 때마다
한 겹씩 옷을 벗고 나서는 구름,
멀리 웃고만 계신 당신 옆모습이랄까?
손 안 닿을 만큼 멀리 빛나는 슬픔의 높이.

3.

아무의 뜨락에도 들어서 보지 못하고
아무의 들판에서 쉬지도 못하고
기웃기웃 여기 다다랐습니다.
고개 들어 우러르면 하늘, 당신의 이마.

4.

호오, 유리창 위에 입김 모으고
그 사람 이름 썼다 이내 지우는
황홀하고도 슬픈 어리석음이여,
혹시 누구 알 이 있을까 몰라⋯⋯.

Autumn Letter • 2

1.

If this sorrow is something even you can't easily lift up

I will go out to the sea and stand at sunset.

To meet the departing rays of sunlight quickly showing their back.

To have the second farewell from the rays of sunlight.

2.

With a blink of an eye or two

Emerging clouds taking off each layer of clothes,

Maybe the profile of your face smiling far away?

The height of sorrow shining too far to reach.

3.

Unable to enter anyone's garden

Unable to rest in anyone's field

I have snooped to arrive here.

Lifting my head to the sky, your forehead.

4.

Hooo, gathering my breaths on the window

I write his name and erase immediately

What ecstatic and sad foolishness,

I wonder if somebody knows it...

단풍

숲속이 다, 환해졌다
죽어 가는 목숨들이
밝혀 놓은 등불
멀어지는 소리들의 뒤통수
내 마음도 많이, 성글어졌다
빛이여 들어와
조금만 놀다 가시라
바람이여 잠시 살랑살랑
머물다 가시라.

Fall Foliage

The forest, has fully brightened

The lamp turned on

By the dying lives

The back of head of the disappearing sound

My mind also, has much ripened

Come, light

And play a while before you go

Winds, gently stay

Before you go.

아침

어제는 던져버리고
오늘은 어느새 새것이다
아, 나도 새것이다

물소리 물소리가 먼저 와
기다리고 있었구나
물소리도 새것이다

풀벌레 소리도 이미 새것
산도, 산의 이마도 새것
나무 나무 나무들도 새것

자, 가보자
오늘도 세상 속으로
독립운동하러 떠나보자.

Morning

Discarding yesterday

Today has arrived anew

Ah, I am also new

The sound of water

Water has been waiting for me already

The sound of water is also new

The sound of insects is already new

The mountain, its forehead is new

The tree tree trees are new

Let's go

Into the world today

Let's depart to declare Independence.

꽃 피는 전화

살아서 숨 쉬는 사람인
것만으로도 좋아요
아믄, 아믄요
그냥 거기 계신 것만으로도 참 좋아요
그러엄, 그러믄요
오늘은 전화를 다 주셨군요
배꽃 필 때 배꽃 보러
멀리 한 번 길 떠나겠습니다.

A Blooming Call

Your being just alive and breathing

Is good enough

Yes, yes

Your being just there is so good

Yes, yes

You even gave me a call today

When pear flowers bloom

I shall go away far to see them.

응?

초록의 들판에
조그만 소년이
가볍게 가볍게
덩치 큰 소를 끌고 가듯이

귀여운 어린 아기가 끌고 가는
착하신 엄마와 아빠

어여쁜 아이들이 끌고 가는
정다운 학교와 선생님

아가야, 지구를 통째로
너에게 줄 테니
잠들 때까지 망가뜨리지 말고
잘 가지고 놀거라, 응?

Okay?

On a green field
Like a small boy
Lightly lightly
Drags a huge ox

Sweet mother and father
Drawn by a cute little baby

An affectionate school and a teacher
Led by adorable children

Baby, I'll give you
This whole earth
Why don't you play with it till bedtime
Without breaking it, okay?

서러운 봄날

꽃이 피면 어떻게 하나요
또다시 꽃이 피면 나는
어찌하나요

밥을 먹으면서도 눈물이 나고
술을 마시면서도 나는
눈물이 납니다

에그 나 같은 것도 사람이라고
세상에 태어나서 여전히 숨을 쉬고
밥도 먹고 술도 마시는구나 생각하니
내가 불쌍해져서 눈물이 납니다

비틀걸음 멈춰 밑을 좀 보아요
앉은뱅이걸음 무릎걸음으로 어느새
키 낮은 봄 풀들이 밀려와
초록의 주단방석을 깔려합니다

일희일비,

조그만 일에도 기쁘다 말하고
조그만 일에도 슬프다 말하는 세상
그러나 기쁜 일보다는
슬픈 일이 많기 마련인 나의 세상

어느 날 밤늦도록 친구와 술 퍼마시고
집에 돌아가 주정을 하고
아침밥도 얻어먹지 못하고 집을 나와
새소리를 들으며 알게 됩니다

봄마다 이렇게 서러운 것은
아직도 내가 살아 있는
목숨이라서 그렇다는 것을
햇빛이 너무 부시고 새소리가
너무 고와서 그렇다는 걸 알게 됩니다

살아 있다는 것만으로도
아, 그것은 얼마나
고마운 일이겠는지요……

꽃이 피면 어떻게 하나요
또다시 세상에 꽃 잔치가 벌어지면
나는 눈물이 나서 어찌하나요.

Spring Sorrow

What shall I do when flowers bloom
When flowers bloom again
What shall I do

Tears are falling while I eat
My tears are falling
While I drink

Gee, even a man like me was born into the world
As a human being and still breathes
Eats rice and drinks wine
Thinking about it makes me shed tears out of pity

Stop stumbling and see under your feet
Already squatting and crawling
Short spring grasses have flooded
Trying to spread a green carpet

The tide of joy and sorrow,

The world that says delight with something small

Sad with something small

But my world that is more inclined to sad things

Than delightful things

One day after heavy drinking with a friend till late at night

Returning home and gibbering

Leaving home without getting any breakfast

I realize while listening to the birds singing

That this much sorrow every spring

Is because I am still

A living being

And because the sunlight is too bright and

The bird songs are too beautiful

Just being alive

Ah, how grateful

That could be…

What shall I do when flowers bloom

When a flower festival opens again in the world

What shall I do with my tears.

멀리까지 보이는 날

숨을 들이쉰다
초록의 들판 끝 미루나무
한 그루가 끌려 들어온다

숨을 더욱 깊이 들이쉰다
미루나무 잎새에 반짝이는
햇빛이 들어오고 사르락 사르락
작은 바다 물결 소리까지
끌려 들어온다

숨을 내어쉰다
뻐꾸기 울음소리
꾀꼬리 울음소리가
쓸려 나아간다

숨을 더욱 멀리 내어쉰다
마을 하나 비 맞아 우거진
봉숭아꽃나무 수풀까지
쓸려 나아가고 조그만 산 하나
우뚝 다가와 선다

산 위에 두둥실 떠 있는
흰구름, 저 녀석
조금 전까지만 해도 내 몸 안에서
뛰어놀던 바로 그 숨결이다.

A Day I Can See Afar

I inhale

From the edge of the green field

An aspen tree is drawn in

I inhale more deeply

The sunlight shining in the aspen leaves

Is pulled in along with

The gentle laps of

The small ocean waves

I exhale

The sound of cuckoo

The sound of oriole

Are washed out

I exhale more deeply

A village even a forest of

Balsam trees lush in rain

Are released and a small mountain

Emerges vividly

The white cloud floating

Over the mountain, that guy

Is the very breath playing

In my body just a while ago.